Dunc's
Halloween

Gary Paulsen

Dunc's Halloween

A YEARLING BOOK

Published by
Dell Publishing
a division of
Bantam Doubleday Dell Publishing Group, Inc.
1540 Broadway
New York, New York 10036

ISBN: 0-440-40659-5

Printed in the United States of America

October 1992

10 9 8 7 6 5 4

OPM

Dunc's
Halloween

Chapter·1

Duncan—Dunc—Culpepper barreled down the alley, his knees coming up past his waist, his arms pumping like pistons. He was frantically chasing his best friend for life, Amos Binder.

It was a Friday, the night before Halloween.

"This way," Amos shouted over his shoulder. "Hurry!"

Dunc pounded with Amos across a street, through someone's garden, and over a fence. He barely escaped being splattered by a dump truck and got shredded when he accidentally stomped on the tail of a very angry tomcat and spindled on the Mackersons' steel picket fence. Finally, just as it seemed his lungs would burst, they collapsed on the front steps of the Kowalskis', panting.

Amos took a stopwatch out of his pocket and studied it under the cold light of a full moon. He shook his head. "Too slow—that took thirty-seven seconds." He wheezed, fighting for breath. "We'll need to cut it down to thirty-five if we want to stay on schedule."

Dunc was blue, fading to red. "Amos, tell me again. Why are we doing this?"

"It will take rehearsal runs to hit all the good candy houses tomorrow night."

"I'd settle for less candy and more breath. My throat feels like someone rubbed it down with oven cleaner."

"No pain, no gain." Amos looked at the watch again. "If I hadn't tripped over the Winterses' garden hose, I think we would have made it." He rubbed his head. "What does it mean, that word Winters yelled at us?"

Dunc shrugged. "I don't know—I've

never heard it before. Something to do with a truck, I think. Or maybe rotten vegetables. The thing you've got to remember is, tomorrow night will be even worse. The streets will be filled with little kids."

"We can hurdle them—two feet, at the most three. It's easy to clear them."

"We'll be carrying bags of candy. That's a lot of extra weight."

"I've got that part all figured out." Amos took a street map out of his pocket. "This red line is our route. See these blue squares?"

"Yeah."

"They're storage points. All we have to do is toss the candy in as we run by. That way we can travel light."

"And you figure we can hit every good place in town?"

"Sure. I've labeled each distance with the minimum amount of time it should take us —if we run fast."

"How fast?"

"Really fast."

"Amos . . ."

"We have to run sixty miles an hour."

3

"Sixty miles an hour? Are you crazy? We can't run that fast!"

Amos shook his head. "Don't be so negative. If we start at exactly eight thirty we'll finish at ten forty-seven. Of course, we'll have to minimize the time we spend at each door—two seconds max—but if we shorten 'trick-or-treat' to 'trick-r-treat,' we can save a tenth of a second per house. We need to reach Mrs. Krippner's house before the late news is over."

Dunc stared at Amos for a moment, then shook his head and sighed. "All right. . . . What happens now?"

"The next stop is the Andersons'—they always have those really good caramel apples. Then comes the Bigelows—they give out the full-size candy bars, not those little dinky ones. After that is Herb and Judy Fenson, they always have . . . oh, wait a minute. We'd better not go there." He took a pen out of his pocket and crossed them off.

"Why not?"

"They're kind of mad at me."

"Kind of?"

"I was out walking Scruff the other day—"

"You were walking Scruff? You two hate each other!" Scruff was the Binder family collie. He spent much of his time trying to take chunks out of Amos.

"I have to walk him because Amy won't."

"I thought she liked to walk Scruff."

"She likes me not liking to walk Scruff more." Amy was Amos's older sister. She felt about Amos the same way most people feel about foot fungus, and she worked hard to find names for him that included the word *butt*. Like *butthead, buttface, buttwad.* Her favorite was *buttbrain,* and she once told Amos that if she had nuclear capabilities, his room would be vaporized.

"Anyway," Amos continued, "we were about two blocks from our house. Exactly six hundred and thirty-seven feet from Melissa's front walk—I've measured it from every angle within a half mile—when I heard a phone ring. It was Melissa's ring. You know, the one ring followed right away by that all-important second ring?"

Dunc nodded. Amos was in love with Melissa. He swore that Melissa's ring was different from everybody else's. Dunc had given up arguing with him about it a long time ago. It didn't pay. Melissa spent almost all of every waking moment not thinking of Amos. As a matter of fact, she did not know Amos at all.

"There was a repairman on the top of the pole in front of Herb and Judy's corner grocery with a phone in his hand. I started up after him as fast as I could—you have to answer before that second ring or you'll lose them—and I forgot that I was still holding Scruff's leash. He came up after me, whining and choking and growling. Halfway up the pole, I let go of the leash so he wouldn't strangle."

"That was nice. Instead of hanging him, you splattered him on the concrete."

"No. He grabbed my pant leg. My belt gave out, and my pants worked like a parachute as he dropped to the ground." Amos shrugged, remembering. "It wasn't Scruff that was the problem—it was the telephone man."

"What happened to him?"

"He saw me scrambling up the pole, and just because I was screaming with my pants off, he thought I was crazy. Some people are such poor judges of character."

Dunc waited. "And?"

"He climbed to the top of the pole to get away from me and tried to balance there."

"Tried?"

"When I reached for the phone, he fell one way and I fell the other. I landed in the Johnsons' compost pile across the street. He fell through the awning of Herb and Judy's, right into the watermelon stand. He goes into surgery tomorrow to get the seeds removed from his ears. They're sprouting."

"Poor guy."

"What about me? I never did get to talk to Melissa, and I'll be spitting compost until I die. What do they put in that stuff, anyway?"

It comes from horses, Dunc thought, then he shook his head. It was better that Amos didn't know.

Dunc studied the map. The red line ran everywhere. It would have been much easier to highlight the places they *weren't* going to go.

"Melissa probably wanted to find out what I'm wearing to the Halloween party tomorrow night. She'll want to recognize me."

"Right." *And the moon,* Dunc thought, *rides on the back of a large turtle.*

A sudden long, lonely howl cut the night.

"What was that?" Dunc asked, shivering.

"I'm not sure I want to know." Amos looked—and tried not to look at the same time—around them on the dark street.

"It sounded like a dog. Sort of." Amos shrugged.

"A dog about as big as a Chevrolet, maybe." Dunc shook his head. "I don't know what it was, but it wasn't a dog." He had been kneeling and he stood up. "Right. Let's go home."

"Home? What about the rest of the route?"

"Forget about the rest of the route."

"But what about the candy?"

"Amos, anything that can howl like that will think *we're* candy. Let's go home."

Amos began to fold the map, then shook his head. "I didn't spend a whole year working on this to get scared away by a big dog." He stood up.

"Amos . . ."

"It should take us forty-two seconds to reach the Andersons'. Let's go."

"Amos—"

But Amos was gone, sprinting down the street. Dunc held back for half a second, shook his head, then followed.

Chapter · 2

Dunc was in midhurdle over a plastic flamingo in the back of Mrs. Rigletti's yard
when he heard the howl again.

It was closer than it had been the first
time.

Much closer.

Again the howl sounded, rattling the few
remaining leaves in Mrs. Rigletti's ash tree.

Amos had frozen next to a tall hedge,
and Dunc took a step to be near him.

"I'm not really happy about this," Amos
whispered.

Dunc nodded, started to say something,
then stopped.

11

Footsteps padded on the opposite side of the hedge—big footsteps. They seemed to echo.

"Dunc, you don't suppose this is somebody playing a joke, do you?"

A huge muzzle came around the end of the hedge, snorting twin jets of steam from the nostrils. Then a head, and yellow-green eyes that looked directly at and through Amos and Dunc. The lips lifted to show a seemingly endless row of daggerlike teeth, and it took Dunc a full second to realize that the eyes were looking *down* on them. Whatever it was, the thing was enormous—a scabby, furry, growling house.

Amos nodded, smiling. "Sure. Look—you can see the line where the rubber mask ends. Right there, in back of the drool. It's all a—"

He pointed with a finger and very nearly lost it. In a spray of saliva the teeth swirled and went for the hand. But at the same time Dunc grabbed Amos by the collar and jerked him backward, and the fangs missed and took off about a two-foot section of hedge as neat as a gas-powered trimmer.

"—joke."

By the second step, Dunc was running, dragging Amos backward.

Time hung for half a second, two. Dunc and Amos were moving. Amos's legs caught up with him and his body wheeled, but his head was still facing back at the monster.

The beast spat bits of the Riglettis' hedge, dropped to all fours, and tore after the boys.

Dunc dug hard with his left foot, feinted to the right, then leaned and angled left, ducking down to dive beneath the hedge. Amos had been looking back, watching the thing gain on them, but when he turned, Dunc was suddenly not there.

"Dunc!"

"Ummph. . . ." Dunc scrabbled through to the other side. "Come left. Hard!"

But it was too late. Amos was already past the point where Dunc had dived. He smelled breath on his neck, hot breath, worse than anchovy-pizza breath. Amos threw another quick look over his shoulder and found himself looking down a throat as big as a tunnel.

He hung a right so fast, it threw the monster off.

"I'll come around." Amos snatched a pink plastic flamingo out of the ground as he passed through the Riglettis' garden and tried to use it as a sword. The monster bit its head off.

"Dunc, help me!" He was angling back around to the hedge where Dunc was waiting by the hole that went through to the other side.

"Dive! When you get here, dive, and I'll grab you!"

Amos took two more giant leaps, shoved the pink flamingo back once more, heard a crunch, and dived for the hole.

And almost made it.

He came in at a slight angle. Because he was off to the side, his front half went through clean, but he jammed at the waist for half a second, his knees wedged in and his butt jammed up in the air.

A perfect target.

The fangs came down in a drooling arc, opened and bared, then slammed shut like a vise, and half of Amos would have been

14

gone, but once more Dunc grabbed him by the collar and jerked him. The teeth all but missed—one fang caught the fleshy part of his rear end and made a small rip through Amos's jeans and cut a little scratch. Like a cork in a bottle, Amos popped through.

"Now!" Dunc snapped. "Now *move!*"

He dragged Amos to his feet as the monster's head came slamming into the hole. It was approximately twenty feet to the Riglettis' backyard ash tree, and Dunc made it in one leap, with Amos flying behind him like a rag.

"Climb!" Dunc screamed, grabbing a limb. "It's our only chance. . . ."

Amos caught the same limb, and they hit the tree like cats chased by dogs.

Even then it wouldn't have worked. It was too close. What saved them was that the beast became stuck momentarily in the hole, couldn't get through, and had to pull out and go around the hedge.

As it was, Amos barely escaped getting another wound in the same place. He heard the jaws snap shut and broke all existing records for tree-climbing by using Dunc's back as a ladder.

Twelve feet up, there was a cross limb, and the boys sat on it, peering down.

"What do you suppose it is?" Amos asked. He had to scoot sideways to avoid sitting where his butt was scratched. "It sort of looks like a dog."

"If you could cross a dog with a crocodile, maybe." Dunc shook his head. "And then it would have to be a very big dog and a very big crocodile."

The beast leaped up at them and the boys jumped, but it missed them by half a foot. Amos was still holding the tattered bits of the plastic flamingo—he'd forgotten to drop it—and he swiped at the monster with the end of it.

For a moment it stood, its head cocked sideways, peering up at them with yellow-green eyes, a low growl rumbling in its throat.

"The eyes," Dunc said. "Isn't there something familiar about them?"

Amos stared down, then shook his head.

16

"I don't see anything there I recognize—or want to recognize."

Again it jumped up at them, and again it was half a foot short. Its claws shredded tree bark on the way down, and this time it lowered to a crouch, growled up at them once more, and with a loping gait disappeared off into the darkness along the hedge and between the houses.

"Gone," Dunc said. "I think it's gone."

Neither boy moved.

"Yup." Amos nodded. "I think you might be right. It's gone."

No movement.

"I guess we could get down," Dunc said.

"Yeah, I guess we could."

Still no movement.

Mrs. Rigletti came out at seven the next morning, just after daylight, to empty her cat box. She was surprised to see Dunc and Amos sitting in the ash tree in her back yard.

"Good morning, Mrs. Rigletti," Amos greeted her. "How are you this morning?"

Mrs. Rigletti stared a them for a full half

minute. Amos was still holding a scrap of her pink plastic flamingo, and her hedge looked as if a buzz saw had hit it.

Her mouth opened, closed, opened and closed again, and she turned back into the house, shaking her head.

She knew about Amos Binder, knew better than to ask questions.

Chapter · 3

Amos awakened just after noon with a funny, dried-out taste in his mouth, as if he'd been panting. After his mother and father had chewed him out for being gone all night and grounded him until sometime after he started shaving, he'd put iodine on the scratch on his rear end and crawled into bed for a nap.

He climbed out of bed and used the mirror over his dresser to examine the scratch again.

It was gone. Completely. There was an iodine stain there, but no scratch, no other

mark of any kind, and even the slight pain
was gone.

"What—"

At that precise moment the phone rang.

Dunc had once tried to calm Amos about
the phone ringing, tried to use logic to show
Amos that it wasn't really necessary to go
totally insane when the phone rang. And
Amos had nodded and agreed, and the next
time the phone rang he had been gone like a
greyhound when a rabbit sped past. He sim-
ply couldn't help it. "I come from a bad gene
pool," he'd told Dunc. "Bad phone genes
back there somewhere."

Phones were located at four strategic
points throughout the Binder home. They
had started with one in the living room and
one in the kitchen. But after Amos had de-
stroyed the upstairs railing trying to get
down by the second ring, his father had put
two more phones upstairs, one by the bathroom door—because he thought Amos spent
so much time in the bathroom—and one
near the top of the stairway. All the phones
had twenty-foot-long coiled cords to give
Amos room to maneuver. In a family confer-

ence Amos's mother—who had already been run over several times—had suggested putting phones every four feet along all the walls, but Amos's father had voted it down as too expensive. Amy, Amos's sister, had wanted to put a phone in the toilet and when he went for it "flush him away," but nobody but Amos had taken her seriously.

Obeying instinct, Amos now made for the phone in the upstairs hall. He showed classic phone-answering form: arms and legs pumping, tongue out to the side, a little spit flying back. There was a good chance he would make it by that all-important second ring.

Or there *would* have been a good chance. Except.

His sweat pants were still down around his ankles because he had been examining the scratch on his rear end.

He was moving forward at close to terminal velocity—or his top half was, but the bottom half couldn't keep up.

He started down.

One scrabbling, clawing hand caught the doorknob and opened the door, and he went through, propelled forward by his tangled, driving legs.

He snagged the phone from the wall on the way past and looked up in horror to see that he was aimed at the open bathroom door—the bathroom was straight across from his room—and worse, at the toilet.

Headfirst.

He slammed the phone to his ear. "Hello . . ."

And was going to add: ". . . Melissa," because he was certain it was she, but the speed with which he was pounding forward and down at the same time drove his head cleanly, perfectly into the toilet.

For a moment it seemed the toilet was going to win. Amos's arms and legs flailed, and the phone flew into the tub, then bounced back as the cord jerked it out into the hallway. In a spray of water Amos fought his way free, scrabbled back into the hallway on all fours, his sweat pants still down around his ankles, and he captured the phone once more.

"Amos—is that you?" Dunc's voice was on the other end.

"Dunc? I was sure it was Melissa."

"I'm sorry. I should have known. How are you doing?"

Amos looked down at the water dripping, pulled his pants up, and stood. "About normal."

"We need to get together."

"I'm grounded. My folks are gone for the day, but I can't leave."

"Grounded? Because a monster kept you in a tree all night?"

"Well . . ."

"Well what?"

"I didn't tell them about the monster. I thought it wouldn't be believable."

Dunc sighed. "Amos—what did you tell your folks?"

"That we were kidnapped by Peruvian money-launderers who needed us to help count drug money."

"And you thought they'd believe *that*?"

"It was all I could think of on short notice. It was better than my second choice— I was going to tell them we'd been kidnapped by a UFO and they held us for hours while they performed unspeakable surgery through our navels with a long needle, trying to learn the secrets of the human race. I just couldn't work it into the conversation."

Dunc snorted. "I don't blame them for grounding you."

Amos shook his head and cleared the water out of his hair and eyes. "What did you mean when you said we have to get together?"

"I've been doing some research down at the library this morning, and I think we may have a problem."

"You mean you got up this morning and went to the library?"

"No. I was up all night, remember? There's something we have to investigate."

"I hate that."

"Hate what?"

"When you say that—'we have to investigate.' I always get in trouble when you say that."

"Not always."

"Always. Every single time. And it's going to happen again, I can feel it."

Dunc ignored him. "When your folks

24

grounded you, did they say you couldn't have company?"

"Not exactly. Dad said I couldn't do anything that was fun for the rest of my life. But that doesn't count here—I'm sure this isn't going to be any fun."

"I'll be right over."

Dunc hung up before Amos could say another word, which was just as well because Amos had been about to tell him not to come.

Amos replaced the phone and moved downstairs. When Dunc said he would be right over, he meant it, and Amos was hungry. As a matter of fact, he felt as if he were starving.

I haven't eaten, he thought, *since I was born. They don't make enough food.*

He moved to the kitchen and opened the refrigerator.

"Leftovers."

Leaning against the door, he polished off a pound of potato salad, half a meat loaf, and a full bowl of macaroni salad.

And he was still hungry.

In the meat tray there was a full pound

of hamburger, extra lean, that his mother was saving for spaghetti that night.

Amos stared at the meat.

Strange, he thought, *how good it looks, lying there, all raw and fresh.* Little bits of blood in it were mixed with pieces of meat and fat, just ground up and waiting. Perfectly good bloody meat, just going to waste.

Amos ate the meat. Raw. The whole pound. And licked the paper wrapper, and when he was finished, he went into the living room to move to the door. Along the way he spied a small rug in the hallway by the door.

Scruff was lying there, his nose curled in under his tail.

Amos moved to stand over the dog.

Scruff looked up, lifted his lip, and growled. There was once a time when Amos would have moved away. Scruff's favorite hobby was removing pieces from Amos.

Now Amos didn't move. He looked down at Scruff. He lifted his lip and growled at the dog.

Scruff's eyes widened. He growled back.

Amos growled louder, made his eyes into

slits, bared his teeth, and felt the hair go up on the back of his neck.

Scruff got up and walked away.

Amos watched him leave, his eyes slitted, a low growl in his throat. Then he lay down on the rug, curled up in a ball with his nose tucked up to his butt and went to sleep.

Chapter · 4

"Amos?"

Dunc stood just inside the door over Amos, who was still curled on the throw rug sound asleep.

"Are you all right?"

Amos opened his eyes sluggishly and looked up.

"Oh—hi, Dunc."

"What are you doing?"

"What do you mean?"

"Down there on the rug. What are you doing?"

Amos sat up, then stood. "I was tired, and the rug looked comfortable. I thought

29

I'd take a little rest. What's wrong with that?"

Dunc studied him, then shook his head. "Nothing—I just thought it was strange."

Amos shrugged. "People get tired—especially after sitting in trees all night. At least normal people do. Not you, of course—what's in the books?"

Dunc was holding a stack of books under his arm. "I brought them from the library. They have more there, but I couldn't check them all out. I told you I was doing research."

"On speed," Amos said, nodding. "How to cut time when we make our candy run tonight. Good thinking. We want to keep up a good lope, get it up around sixty, or we'll lose out. I wonder if any of them give meat for a treat."

Dunc had started for the stairs and hadn't heard Amos. "Come on up to your room—you've got to see this."

Amos followed, dropping to all fours while he went up the stairs behind Dunc. His shoulders rolled easily while he moved.

He stood upright at the top of the stairs and followed Dunc into his room.

"Man, you should do something about this place." Dunc stopped inside the door.

"You've seen it before."

"I know, but it's always a shock."

Amos's room looked exactly as if somebody had thrown a grenade into it, then closed the door. Maybe two grenades. Perhaps, Dunc had once said, a bombing raid.

Once a week, forced by his parents, he pretended to clean it. He jammed everything under the bed. This had worked for a while, but after weeks, months, years, the bed couldn't take it any longer. There were still toys beneath his bed from the time before he could talk, toys with rattles on them, jammed together with old dirty socks and underwear, a food container that had once held a cheese dip and that had grown and grown until it was almost alive, and Dunc swore that either the old underwear or the dip container had learned to growl if anybody looked beneath the bed.

Around the room were posters, models

31

hanging from the ceiling, and the smell of—well, as Dunc said, everything.

Dunc's room was always clean and orderly.

"Clear a place on the bed," Amos said. "Spread the books there."

Amos cleared the bed—a yo-yo, a slingshot, and a skateboard without wheels were there—and Dunc put the books down.

"I started thinking after I got home. Thinking about that—that thing that put us up the tree," Dunc said. "I thought it might be some kind of wolf, you know, because it was bigger than a dog and had a kind of long snout."

He paused. "I did a little checking on wolves at the library. Did you know that they don't get as big as the one we saw last night? They don't get much larger than a big dog. And their geographical range doesn't extend this far south. There's never been a substantiated attack of a healthy wolf on a human in North America."

"How can you use words like that?"

"What word?"

"*Substantiated.* I mean, how come you

use words like that, and I don't even *think* those kinds of words?"

Dunc shrugged. "I don't know. I guess from reading in the library. What difference does it make? The main thing is, I don't think it was a wolf. So I started digging further, and I came up with some pretty strange things."

An itch took Amos. Not just an itch, but the biggest itch of all time. Just in back of his ear. He'd never felt an itch like this, not even close. He scratched with his right hand, scratched and scratched, and it felt so good, soooo verrrry gooood.

His right foot started to thump on the floor.

"Amos," Dunc stared at his foot. "What are you doing?"

"Unnnnhhhhhh . . . scratching." He stopped scratching, and the leg stopped. "Why?"

"You just seem to be doing it a strange way." Dunc shrugged. "I thought . . ." He shook his head. "Never mind. Now look at this."

He turned back to the books.

33

"None of it made sense—the way the thing looked, the way it came after us, until I remembered there was a full moon last night."

Amos nodded. "Yeah, it was full. So what does that mean?"

Dunc looked at Amos, waiting.

Nothing came.

"Put it together," Dunc said. "Something sort of like a wolf, a full moon . . ."

"Oh." Amos nodded. "You mean were-wolves. That's fine for movies and stuff, but it isn't real. I don't know what that thing was, but it was real."

"There's real," Dunc said, "and then there's real."

"What is that supposed to mean?"

"It means," Dunc said, opening a book, "that we don't know all there is to know about the phenomenon of lycanthropy. Look—"

"I hate that, when you use big words," Amos said. But he looked.

"People have been scared of wolves for a long time," Dunc said. "Without reason. They've almost always kept to themselves.

34

But the fear was so great that they transferred it to anybody who even started to act a little weird. They said they maybe had been bitten by a wolf and then had turned into a wolf."

Amos was reading ahead of Dunc. "It says it's all a bunch of old superstitions."

Dunc nodded. "I read that. But there are several cases that aren't so easy to explain. Some guy in Hungary back about three hundred years ago was caught running nude through the woods with a pack of wolves, and they said he could change into one whenever he wanted."

"And you think that monster after us last night was a werewolf?"

Dunc shook his head. "Not necessarily. It just might have been somebody who *thinks* he's a werewolf."

Amos looked at Dunc for a long time. "It bit a plastic flamingo completely in half, Dunc—like it was snapping off a Twinkie. It had teeth you could use for floor lamps, Dunc. That wasn't imaginary."

"Yes, it might have been. People do strange things—they can rip a car door off, if they panic. It happens all the time. If they're hysterical or in a trance, they can do lots of weird things. A good mask, some hair glued on a body—I tell you, I recognized those eyes. That was somebody we know."

"It was?"

"I'm sure of it. All we have to do is figure out who it was and cure him, and that will be the end of it."

"Cure him? They have pills for this?"

Dunc picked up a book, thumbed to a place he had marked with a piece of notebook paper, and opened it. "It's the same as the problem—if they *think* they can be cured of the imaginary problem, then it cures them. One psychiatrist used a silver butter knife and cured somebody of imaginary werewolfism. Just scratched him on the forehead three times."

"So all we do is find this thing," Amos said, "go up to it—that is get really close to it, right in its face—and scratch it three times with a butter knife."

"Right."

"Wrong." Amos shook his head. "Not for anything. Not for a date with Melissa. Not for a single thing in the whole world am I going to try and scratch that thing with a butter knife. Not me, not ever. You might, but not me."

Dunc ignored him. "It has to be tonight. Halloween. It's the last full moon for another month. We'll have to get you off being grounded and find it tonight."

"You're forgetting trick or treats, and after that there's the Halloween costume party. Melissa's going to be there. I'll skip my grounding if I have to, but I'm not missing it."

But Dunc still didn't hear him. "Yeah. He'll be out tonight, sure as anything. We'll set a trap for him, catch him, and cure him."

"I was going as a groom," Amos said. His voice was sad because he knew now that he would have to help Dunc. He would never get out of it. "I thought if she saw me as a groom, maybe—"

"Some kind of trap. That's the problem: How do you trap a werewolf?"

Chapter · 5

"You know, everybody has it wrong. They all think *I'm* the crazy one, but it's not me—it's you."

Amos was standing in his room with a costume on.

He looked like a sheep.

Dunc was pulling here and there, trying to make it fit better. It was a bit small. "It was the closest the costume store had to a sheep—and we were lucky to get it, considering it's Halloween. It's made for a small child. Maybe if you stayed on all fours it would hold its shape. Try it."

He pushed Amos down.

"Dunc . . ."

"Be quiet now. Let me look."

Dunc stood back. Amos looked like somebody's idea of a cartoon lamb. The suit stuck out here and there. Odd bits of wool were glued to the lining, and it had flopping ears and a long tail.

"Perfect."

"You're lying," Amos said. "I can tell by your voice. That tone means you're lying. I don't look at all like a sheep. I look like a ruptured llama."

"But in the dark or in the full moon, it'll work. I know it. One of the articles said that werewolves like sheep more than anything."

"When you say *like,* you actually mean they like to *attack* sheep, don't you?"

Dunc nodded. "Small point. Yes. But we'll have him long before then. I'm going to use our old volleyball net and stretch it across that opening back of the Riglettis'. You pretend to be grazing there, in the Riglettis' back yard, and when he comes for you, I'll spring the net on him. Then I'll scratch him with the butter knife, and it'll all be over. Piece of cake."

Amos stood. "Don't say that—about it being a piece of cake. That's the jinx saying. When you say that, it always goes wrong. I'll do this, but don't say that."

"You're being negative," Dunc said. "Remember to stay positive. Be grateful. Look how we got you out of being grounded."

Amos nodded. "You told the truth. Heck, if I'd known that would work on my folks, I would have done it long ago."

"But you should still be grateful."

Amos nodded. "I am." He started taking the suit off.

"What are you doing?"

"Dunc, it's two in the afternoon. We can't do this until tonight, and I'm not going to keep the suit on all day. I'll rot."

"Oh." Dunc nodded. "I just thought we could sit around and watch the sunset and wait for the moon to change."

"No."

"How about if we go back to the library and see if there are any more books on werewolves?"

Amos dropped the sheep suit in a lump.

41

"Only if we can go past Melissa's house. It's only three hundred and forty-seven feet out of the way from the straight route between here and the library."

Dunc sighed. "All right."

"I thought I might get a chance to see her through a window and see what costume she's wearing to the costume party tonight."

"I understand," Dunc said, although in truth he didn't.

Amos headed for the door, and Dunc held back to take a moment to straighten out the sheep suit and lay it on the bed. The re-arranged suit made the rest of the bed look messy, so he took an extra moment to re-make the bed. The neatened bed made the rest of the room look like a disaster area, so he added a minute to straighten out some of the pictures and clear away the rubble on top of the desk, where there were some pen-cils that needed sharpening in the sharp-ener bolted to the side of the window, and the sharpened pencils made all the papers look completely goobered up, and he took another minute . . .

42

"WILL YOU COME *ON!*" Amos screamed from the door. "You're driving me nuts with this."

Dunc jumped and followed Amos out the door.

Outside, it was a spectacular fall day. The sun was bright and the air was crisp. All the elms and oaks were changing colors, and in the afternoon sun the street looked bathed in color.

"I feel good about tonight," Amos said. Dunc was walking down the sidewalk, but Amos trotted out ahead, then went around Dunc and got in front of him, trotting backward so he could talk.

"So do I," Dunc said. "I think we have a real good chance to catch the werewolf."

"Not that." Amos shook his head. "I mean I feel good about the costume party and Melissa and all. If I close my eyes, I can see how it will go—you know, the way you do? Where you see it all the way it's supposed to happen? I'll come in and Melissa will be there, maybe bobbing for apples. I'll lower my head underwater, and we'll see

43

each other through the floating apples, and she'll know—"

He stopped talking suddenly, stopped dead in front of Dunc so abruptly that Dunc ran into him.

"Amos—"

"Cat." Amos raised his head, turned it, his nostrils quivering. "I smell a cat. Close, too. And on the ground. Smells like a big tom."

"Amos?" Dunc looked at him. "Are you all right?"

Amos ignored him. "Close . . . very close . . ."

Mrs. Shandorf lived in the house four doors down from Amos's place. She was a nice older woman, widowed, and she spent a lot of her time trying to make an old alley cat she'd adopted weigh more than a car. She named the cat Iver and fed it constantly, and it had grown and grown until it weighed close to forty pounds. Scarred and mangy from a million alley-cat fights, Iver spent most of his time hiding in the Shandorf rose bushes waiting for unsuspecting cats or small dogs to come by. Iver would jump them with glee, trying his best to pound them into mush.

"It's Iver," Amos said. "See him, hiding under the rose bush there? He thinks we can't see him. Man, a chance to get Iver . . ."

"Amos—"

But Amos was gone. In a sudden lope he made for the hedge where Iver was hiding, growling low in his throat.

Iver spent half a second wondering just exactly why a boy he'd seen every day of his life walking past the yard had suddenly turned into a raving maniac and was coming at him like a Doberman.

It very nearly cost him.

With bared teeth and the growl changing to a snarl, Amos came within an inch of catching him.

At the last possible second Iver made up his mind and exploded out of the rose bush, back down the narrow slot between Mrs. Shandorf's house and the next one.

The sudden maneuver threw Amos half a step off, but he countered by throwing his weight sideways and made the turn, following Iver down between the buildings.

He was gaining.

"Amos?" Dunc was still standing on the sidewalk, his hand half raised, speaking to the empty spot where Amos had been just a second before. "Are you all right?"

Amos was already beyond earshot.

Iver heard the pounding feet in back of him, heard them gaining, and he added a few miles an hour to his stride. The space between the buildings was long, and at the end there was a small, low shed that held gardening tools.

Iver put everything into his legs and made one huge leap to clear the building.

But he was fat, very fat, and his weight held him down. He made the slanted metal roof, but he failed to clear it and slid for a moment trying to get purchase.

Amos was on him. He took a bite at the big cat's rump. Iver broke free and over the roof and was gone.

Amos looked at the building, ran back and forth whining for a moment, then trotted back out to where Dunc still stood, his hand raised, staring at Amos.

Amos spat cat hair out. "I almost had him. I mean, it was *that* close. Next time he's mine."

"Amos . . ."

Amos looked at Dunc. "What's the matter? Haven't you ever seen a cat before?"

Dunc nodded. "Well, yes. But I've never seen you chase and bite at one."

Amos spat the last of the cat hair out. "It's all a matter of attitude."

"Attitude?"

"Yeah. I mean Iver, you know—what a snot. Every day I walk by, and he sits there like he owns the world, just sits there with that superior attitude like he's better than dogs. He thinks I don't know what he's thinking, but I do know what he's thinking, and I think it stinks, what he's thinking. I think his thinking attitude needs changing. So I went for him."

"So you went for him. . . ."

"Almost had him, too. Man, I'd like nothing better than to put him up a tree and

47

keep him there for an hour or two while he adjusts his attitude. Well, maybe next time. Come on—don't you want to get to the library?"

He trotted off down the street, moving easily on the outsides of his feet, his shoulders rolling freely. Dunc started after him.

They'd gone almost a block before Dunc realized he had to run nearly wide open just to keep up with Amos.

"Hey, hold up."

Amos turned, his tongue hanging out a bit, panting easily while he ran. "What's the matter?"

"I can't keep up."

"But we're just trotting."

"You are. I'm running flat out, and you're just pooping along. I don't understand it. And why are you panting?"

Amos shrugged. "I don't know. I felt a bit warm and thought it might cool me off."

"Amos, aren't you acting a bit strange?"

Amos stopped and scratched himself in back of the ear. "I don't think so. Wait—look! It's a UPS truck. Oh, man, I can't stand those things—"

He turned away from Dunc and shot out into the street, tearing after the UPS truck.

Dunc stopped and stood watching him run after the back tire on the truck.

"Amos?"

Chapter·6

They stopped only briefly at Melissa's house. Amos didn't even look in the window. He took one whiff of the front sidewalk and shook his head.

"She's not here. Been gone a little over an hour, maybe an hour and four minutes. Let's go." He moved off down the street, trotting.

Dunc trailed along, shaking his head. None of it made sense.

Amos had chased the UPS truck for a full two blocks while Dunc stared after him. And Amos had almost caught it, showing what he would have called classic form, both legs pumping, a bit of spit flying, lips bared, and throat in a low growl. When he was close to the tire, the truck had taken a sudden left and Amos had missed, swung around to the right, and trotted back to Dunc as though everything were normal.

"Did you see that? I just missed him. It must be my day for just missing—first Iver, and now the UPS truck."

Dunc had stopped him. "Amos, is there something you aren't telling me?"

"About what?"

"Anything. You're chasing cats and UPS trucks and sleeping on little rugs in your hallway."

But Amos had wheeled away and set off at an easy trot headed for Melissa's, and Dunc had to run to catch up.

But it still bothered him.

Now, heading for the library after they'd found that Melissa wasn't home, Dunc tried to puzzle it out again.

"It's all very mysterious," he mumbled aloud.

Amos was well ahead, half a block at least, and he turned and came back at a fast lope, his tongue hanging out in a soft pant. "What's mysterious?"

"You heard me say that?"

"Sure. You practically yelled it."

But I didn't, Dunc thought. *I whispered it, and he was half a block away.* "Everything about this Halloween is weird. We see that monster last night, and now you're acting so strange."

"I'm not acting strange."

"You are. You're acting just like a—well, a dog."

"You're nuts." They were near the park across from the library, and Amos took off at a run through a flock of pigeons in front of the statue of a Civil War hero named Thromborton who had done something terribly important that nobody could remember. The pigeons flew up in a scattering cloud, and Amos circled back to Dunc.

"Don't you love that—the way they fly up and head off in all directions? I just love that. It's almost as good as cats and UPS trucks."

Dunc shook his head and seemed about to say something, but they were at the library steps and they went inside before he could talk.

Dunc loved the library. It was an old building, with high old-fashioned ceilings and tall wooden shelves. He sometimes liked to go and just stand back there in the books and feel them in his mind.

Amos thought he was nuts. Or he always had before.

This time he stopped just inside the door. "The smells."

"What?" Dunc stopped next to him.

"Old smells. Smell them? Old wood and leather, old smells of oil, rich smells—makes me think of old nice things. I never knew how neat the library was—I never really smelled it before. Oh, wait—something else. There are two people in here who really need a shower."

"Amos, we have to talk. Come on."

Dunc led him back into a room where there were typewriters on tables. With the computers up front, nobody ever used the typewriters anymore, so the room was almost always empty, as it was now.

"Somebody was here less than half an

hour ago," Amos said. "Chewing bubble gum. You know, the fruity kind. It was a girl. And she had just about chewed the gum completely—maybe ten more bites, and the sweetness would all be gone."

Dunc sat Amos in a chair by a typewriter. "All right—what's different with you?"

Amos shook his head. "Like I said—nothing. I'm fine."

Dunc nodded. "Maybe, but you're totally different. And we have to find out why. Let's go back over the last twenty-four hours."

Amos shrugged. "We've been together all the time. Yesterday we flummoxed around the mall a little. Then it got dark, and we tried our test run for trick or treat. Then we got jumped by the monster and you deserted me when I got stuck in the hedge, and he bit me in the butt and—"

Dunc stopped him. "Wait. Right there. What was that?"

"You deserted me in the hedge."

"No, after that. Something about the monster."

"I got stuck in the hedge, and he bit me in the butt."

"The monster bit you?"

Amos shook his head. "It wasn't much of a bite. He nailed me just as I was getting through and made a tiny scratch in my rear end. It didn't even show this morning when I looked in the mirror, so it couldn't have been much."

Dunc frowned. "Think, now. Did it break the skin?"

Amos shook his head. "I don't think so. It ripped my pants a little, but there wasn't any blood or anything. What's the big deal?"

"Wait here." Dunc went to a back shelf in the nonfiction section and came back with a book. "I couldn't take it out so it's still here." He riffled through the pages. "Here it is: 'It was widely thought that if one was bitten by a werewolf, the disease would be passed with the bite to the person bitten.'"

Amos looked at Dunc. "So what are you telling me—that I'm a werewolf?"

Dunc shook his head. "I don't really believe in all this—not exactly. But if the monster thought he was a werewolf and you

56

subconsciously believed that he thought he was a werewolf, you might think the bite would work enough for it to affect you."

But Amos wasn't listening. He perked up his ears and turned to the front of the library. "She's here."

"Who?"

"Melissa. She just walked in."

Dunc looked at the door to the typing room. It was closed. There was no way Amos could see out into the library. "How can you tell?"

"I smelled her." Amos stood. "She had oatmeal with cinnamon for breakfast, and she brushed with that new toothpaste with the red stripes. I smelled it before at her house. Are we done talking? I want to ask her about the costume party tonight."

And he left the room before Dunc could tell him about his theory. About how Amos maybe hadn't gotten enough of a bite to make him a full werewolf. Maybe only a little bit of a bite only caused a little bit of a reaction.

Not a full werewolf.

Maybe, Dunc thought, watching Amos

trot out of the typing room and into the main part of the library, maybe just enough of a bite to make Amos into just exactly what he seemed to be.

A werepuppy.

Chapter · 7

As it happened, Amos didn't get to speak to Melissa. He came closer than usual, but he didn't break his previous record. The record was from the time she had thought Amos was his cousin, Lash Malesky, the world-class skateboarder. Melissa had actually spoken directly to him that time, but she didn't know it was Amos and so it didn't count.

This time it was very, very close.

Melissa was with a girl named Ehhrim, a black girl who had been born in Ethiopia and moved to the United States two years earlier. She was tall and fine boned and looked like a model. She and Melissa were best friends, and they were in the library so Ehhrim could show Melissa a picture of an Ethiopian dress like the one her mother was making for her to wear to the costume party.

Amos worked out his plan as he left the typing room. He headed across the main lobby of the library to where Melissa and Ehhrim were looking at a computer screen to locate the book.

His plan was simple, and Amos felt it was bound to work.

He would walk right up, say hi, then flat-out ask Melissa what she was wearing, so he could tailor his own costume to fit. A clean, simple plan.

And later, when he and Dunc were talking about it and helping to clean up the library, even Dunc had to admit that it had started out all right. Or appeared to.

Amos walked across the lobby perfectly. Good form, a little bounce in his step, his ears perked up, and his nose twitching as he checked odors. He moved up in back of Melissa and Ehhrim, and opened his mouth and said, "Hi, Melissa. What are you wear—"

He was going to say: What are you wearing to the costume party?

The problem was Harvey.

Two years before Amos and Dunc were born, somebody had dropped a kitten in a box in front of the library.

It had been so cute, the librarian had adopted it and named it Harvey, after a cousin of hers who had also been cute when he was young. Harvey the kitten had turned into Harvey the cat, then Harvey the old library cat. Newspapers had run stories on him, television had come to film him, and though he had about the same personality as a large fur-covered paperweight, everybody who came to the library loved him. They had taken up a collection to give Harvey his own little swinging pet door at the back of the library and a bed and special feeding and watering bowl so he would stop drinking out of the toilets.

Harvey had been out all day, and his odor that lingered in the library wasn't fresh, and Amos had overlooked it in his excitement over speaking to Melissa.

But now Harvey was coming home. Just at the moment Amos was about to speak to Melissa, Harvey came through the pet door, lumbered into the lobby, trotted across the floor, and jumped up onto the main desk to get his daily petting from the librarian.

They were wrong, later, when they said Amos had gone insane. He wasn't insane as much as he was just very, very interested.

What he wound up saying to Melissa was: "Hi, Melissa, what are you wear—*cat!*"

And he was gone, growling and snarling.

During his many years of daily prowling, Harvey had learned how to survive. Without hesitation he leaped from the main desk to the top shelves in the fiction section. Amos went after him.

Shelves, books, and busts of Dickens, Twain, and Shakespeare went flying.

Harvey made one complete circuit of the library on the tops of the shelves, with Amos clawing along just four inches from his tail.

Then Harvey pulled a hard right

through the magazine rack, dipped beneath a potted plant, and made for his pet door in a straight line across the copier and an assistant librarian named Wilson who screamed, "Mad dog! Call the pound!" before going down in a welter of overdue notices.

Amos had been gaining slightly, and as with Iver, he would have had Harvey except for bad luck. He slipped a little, stepped on Wilson, and hit the pet door off balance. He didn't fit through it and jammed headfirst, and his teeth snapped shut just millimeters from Harvey's retreating rear end.

The library stood in stunned silence, looking as if an earthquake had hit. The whole thing hadn't taken five seconds, and the only sound now was Amos jerking and scrabbling to get his head out of the pet door.

"Who was that?" Ehhrim asked Melissa.

"I haven't the slightest," Melissa answered, shaking her head. "Somebody with serious mental problems."

"He spoke to you."

"I can't help that," Melissa said, peering

toward the back of the library, where Amos was struggling with the pet door. "It's sad, isn't it, that people like that are on the streets? They should be in, you know, homes or institutions or something."

Dunc helped Amos pull his head out of the pet door so they could clean the library up. After jerking him out, Amos stood up and straightened his clothes. "I think that went well, don't you? I mean, up to a point."

Dunc looked at the library, at Amos's clothes—which were torn and hanging in rags—and nodded. "Up to a point. Why don't we clean up now and go home?"

Amos nodded. "I'll wait for Melissa to call. . . ."

"Yes," Dunc said, leading Amos to the fiction section to begin reshelving books. "That might be better."

Chapter · 8

The moon showed a crack of silver blue through the east window of Amos's room.

In the time between the destruction of the library and the evening, Dunc had refined the plan.

"It has to be simple."

"Right." Amos nodded. "Like, let's not do it—how's that for simple?"

Dunc shook his head. "Here I am, trying to make you famous—"

"You're trying to make me a lamb chop, that's what you're trying to do."

"Come on, you know I wouldn't do anything that would really hurt you."

Amos just ignored that one. It was too ridiculous to even notice. They were sitting on Amos's bed getting ready to get ready to go to the costume party.

Dunc continued. "We skip trick or treats—"

"*Skip* trick or treats? After I worked on that schedule for weeks? We can make our candy ration for a year if we work it right."

"Think now," Dunc said, holding up his hand. "The neighborhood will be crawling with little kids, and we're going to try trap a werewolf. Or at least somebody who thinks he's a werewolf. It will be too confusing, too dangerous. We have to wait, hold back until after the costume party, then set our trap. If we're out there rumbling around before we're ready to trap him, he might get suspicious and we'll lose our chance."

As always, Dunc talked Amos into it. What was worse, at least to Amos, Dunc also talked him into going to the costume party dressed in his lamb suit. Now he was dragging him out of the house, and they were on their way to the gymnasium.

"Oh, man," Amos said, trotting along

next to Dunc. "This is really bad. I look like I've been hit by a car—like a roadkill somebody scraped up."

"No, you don't. It's cute, really. Melissa will love it. Besides, there wouldn't have been time to change after the party."

They were walking along the sidewalk heading for the costume party. Dunc was dressed as a shepherd, to go with Amos's lamb costume.

Amos stopped dead. "Dunc, you're always telling me to stop and think. All right, now you do it. Think what you're actually doing here."

"What do you mean?"

"You're walking along the street with somebody dressed in a lamb suit, talking about trying to catch a werewolf in a volleyball net."

Dunc looked at Amos. "So?"

"Well, doesn't that sound a little strange to you?"

Dunc thought a moment, then scratched his head. "No—not if we catch him. It will be a first. And besides, I'm prepared." He dug into his pocket and held up something shining silver in the streetlight. "I have the butter knife."

"Oh." Amos nodded. "Oh, good. I feel much better now. I was really worried, but now it's all right. . . ." He trailed off as they approached the gym.

There were monsters and princesses and vampires and pirates and rock stars streaming in from all directions. Amos moved off to the side in the dark place next to the entrance to the gym. "Let's hold back. I want to see if I can recognize Melissa."

Dunc stood next to him. "We don't know what her costume is."

As Dunc studied each person going in the door, his attention was diverted from Amos. Which was just as well.

Back in the shadows, some very strange things were happening to Amos.

The moon had come up over the gym, and as they had walked to the door, Amos had come into the silver-blue light.

The changes came slowly at first, almost not there at all.

He crouched a little. Then a little more. And then his ears and nose grew a little.

Then a little more. And hair grew on his hands and neck and face. Then a little more. And all of this happened and kept happening until it wasn't Amos standing in the dark next to Dunc. It wasn't really *not* Amos, but it wasn't really *him,* either.

The crouch continued until it was just more comfortable for Amos to be down on all fours, while his growing nose made it easier for him to growl and pant than to talk. It all seemed so natural, and it happened one-thing-to-another until Amos wasn't much like Amos any longer. He looked less and less like Amos and more and more like a kind of rangy cross between a coyote and a dog pound stray.

Except, of course, that he was wearing a T-shirt, a pair of Fruit of the Loom shorts, a moldy lamb costume, and a pair of tennis shoes.

Dunc turned. "Amos?"

But Amos was gone. He had dropped back into the darkness, flipped his feet to get the tennis shoes off his paws, and set off at a lope, the lamb costume trailing along behind.

Dunc looked to his right. Amos moved around to his left, zigzagged through some people in costumes, and whipped into the gym.

Dunc didn't see him. "Amos? Come on now. This is no time for kidding around."

Dunc heard a sudden commotion inside the gym, yelling and noise, and he turned to the door.

"Somebody catch him!" an adult voice roared. It was one of the teachers who were chaperoning the party. "They aren't supposed to be in here!"

Dunc moved inside the gym. At first he couldn't see anything through the people milling around.

Then he caught a glimpse of a furry animal zipping through legs and outstretched arms.

Somebody's dog had gotten into the gym, he thought. But something in him knew what it really was even then.

"It's a dog!" someone yelled. "Wearing a costume—a dog. Catch it, catch it!"

That was when Dunc got a clear view

and saw that the "dog" was wearing a tattered lamb suit.

Dunc moved closer, fighting his way through the crowd.

"It's all right, don't worry—I've got him."

The voice was very familiar. Dunc worked his way to where everybody was standing around in a circle and saw Melissa kneeling on the ground.

She was holding the dog, looking up at the rest of them. "He's very friendly."

"Amos?" Dunc said.

Amos wagged his tail at Dunc, panted a bit, and leaned in to let Melissa hug him.

"Oh, man," Dunc said. "We've got to get you out of here."

Amos raised his lips, showed a good set of yellow-white fangs to Dunc, and growled, pushing harder against Melissa.

"Is this your dog?" Melissa asked.

"Well, sort of—yes."

"And you think it's cute to dress him up like this and bring him to a costume party?" Melissa shook her head. "For shame—it takes away his natural dignity."

Dunc looked helplessly at Amos. "If you

don't get out of here, you might, you know, start to change back."

Amos's head sagged.

"What are you talking about?" Melissa asked.

"Now!" Dunc said, pointing to the door. "Right now!"

Amos detached himself from Melissa and slunk toward the gym door through the crowd.

"Good dog," Dunc said, walking beside him. "That's a good dog."

"I think it's awful." Melissa was following next to Amos. "He's so cute!"

Amos wagged his tail and looked up at Melissa with pleading eyes.

"Out!" Dunc said. "Keep going!"

To the door, through the door. Once they were outside, Dunc led the way off into the darkness next to the gym and away from people watching. When they were in the clear, he stopped Amos.

"Hold it right there."

Amos stopped and looked up at Dunc, panting gently, his tail wagging slowly from beneath the lamb costume.

"Can you understand me?" Dunc asked. "You know, like you're a person?"

Amos nodded.

"Good. And can you talk?"

Amos shook his head slowly from side to side. Then he hesitated and bent his tongue and lips and gave it a try.

A muffled whine came out.

"So," Dunc said. "At least you know what I'm saying. Apparently that werewolf got you hard enough to cause a change. As you can tell, you've become a dog. Or a coyote with mange."

Amos growled.

"Well, not that bad—but sort of ugly."

Another growl.

"Here's what we're going to do," Dunc said, reaching inside his shepherd robe and pulling out the silver butter knife. "I'll scratch you on the forehead with this. According to my research, you'll be back to normal in a short time." With his other hand he crossed his fingers.

Amos nodded.

Dunc reached down with the butter

knife, placed the point against Amos's forehead, and began to scratch.

Or was about to begin to.

Amos suddenly went stiff like a poker, swiveled his head, and raised one leg, staring off into the darkness by the Dumpster.

"You're pointing?" Dunc said. "Is that what you are, a bird dog?"

He turned to look.

And found himself staring into two glowing yellow eyes that seemed about a foot apart.

"It's the werewolf," he said. But it was a totally needless comment. By the time the sentence was finished, the monster was on them.

Chapter · 9

"Run, Amos!" Dunc yelled—another needless command. Amos had dodged left, feinted right, and jumped straight in the air, and when he hit the ground, his feet—all four of them—were moving forward at close to the sixty miles an hour he would have liked for trick or treating.

The monster hesitated, and the hesitation saved Dunc. In midstride it made for Amos, then back to Dunc, and finally tore off after Amos.

"Lead him to the Riglettis'!" Dunc screamed at the disappearing Amos. "I'll take a short cut."

He had no way of knowing if Amos had heard him, and it was silly to think of Amos leading the werewolf anywhere.

Amos was just trying to stay alive. While Dunc cut through the alleys to make the two blocks to the Riglettis', where the volleyball net was stretched, Amos tried to stay in front of the monster.

At first it looked bad. The werewolf was gaining.

Then it looked worse than bad. Amos could feel hot breath on his tail, and he knew that in another leap it would be on him.

Just as he moved out of sight of Dunc, as he was heading around the block that Dunc was cutting off by using the alley, at exactly the point where the monster would have had him, Amos found salvation.

They were moving along an old-fashioned picket fence, and at the end three boards were missing.

Amos threw himself at the opening. The monster hit in back of him and burst through, but the tight fit slowed him.

Amos gained two steps, then another

half a step. He bored around the side of the house, back between the houses.

A board fence. He gathered, leaped, and cleared the top, landing in a back yard. He still hadn't put the picture together, didn't know for certain where he was, until he landed in the yard.

In the moonlight he could see that it was full of mounds and holes. That was enough.

It was the Helmut place.

Helmut was a bachelor who lived alone, and from what rumor said, he hadn't cleaned his house since sometime just before the Second World War. But it wasn't his hygiene that worried Amos.

Helmut had two dogs.

Sort of dogs.

At some point somebody had given Helmut two pit bulls, which he had tried to raise as pets. Which was about like raising two Tasmanian devils as pets.

They were completely vicious and spent all their time fighting each other and digging holes looking for something to fight and rip to pieces and kill and eat and chew up and spit out and maim and dismember.

After due consideration, Helmut had named the dogs Death and Destruction. The names fit.

They were not asleep, the pit bulls. Some people said they never slept but sat staring at each other with raging red eyes. Amos landed at a point almost exactly between them.

They saw him at the same instant, but out of disbelief—nothing had ever been crazy enough to actually jump into their yard—they did not react at once.

Which gave the werewolf the moment it needed to clear the fence and land almost perfectly on top of Amos.

In that same split moment the two pit bulls, with grand, grateful snarls, threw themselves through the air. They too landed on Amos.

And the werewolf.

In reality, the fight that ensued could not be measured, and it is not possible to say who won.

Only who lost.

Amos.

The fight had a life of its own. It became

a thing alive. In a great, snarling, rolling, screaming ball the fight tumbled across the yard, slammed against the back fence gate and broke through, boiled and hammered and bled and foamed down the alley with pit bulls first on top, then on the bottom, and the werewolf first on top, then on the bottom, and Amos always, always, on the bottom of it all.

It could not be said that Amos guided the whole screaming mass toward the Riglettis'. Amos was just trying to survive. The fight was so savage and confusing that, at one point, frenzied, he found himself chewing on his own foot.

But the fight did move, it rolled and tumbled and seethed down the alley, and the direction it moved was toward the Riglettis'. When it was at the back of the Riglettis' yard, it seemed to turn or roll sideways and head into the back yard, where it boiled almost directly on top of the waiting Dunc.

With a mighty heave, Dunc pulled the release rope that dropped the volleyball net on all of them. It went down in a rush of screams, growls, bellows, slashing fangs, and the flash of silver as Dunc stabbed and cut at anything that moved with the butter knife.

Chapter · 10

"Don't pick at it." Dunc's voice was muffled through the bandages. "You'll get infected."

"You sound like my mother." Amos could hardly be understood himself. His entire body was wrapped in white strips of tape.

After the police came—called by Mrs. Rigletti—and the ambulances had taken them away, the boys had spent two days in the hospital, mostly getting stitches and shots. They were now at home, and their parents had let them spend the week they would have to stay in bed at Dunc's house together wrapped in bandages and tape.

"Funny how things turn out, isn't it?" Dunc said.

"Oh, yes, hilarious. It's all I can do to stop laughing."

Amos had gotten the worst of it by far—one of the doctors in the emergency room said he looked like a jumbo burger before it's cooked. He was having trouble seeing any humor in any of it.

"No, really. Look at it, and you'll see how crazy it all is." Dunc tried to ease his arm at the place where the rope from the volleyball net had wrapped and burned it when the werewolf had hit the end of the net. "Nobody knows anything about the werewolf business—they just thought all the damage was done by Death and Destruction. That they had gotten out of the yard on their own. So we don't have to explain everything."

"What about Mr. Nerkovich?" Amos asked.

Mr. Nerkovich was the social-studies-teacher-slash-football-coach. That was how he introduced himself—as a social-studies-teacher-slash-football-coach. Everybody called him Slash. It was he who had been the original werewolf. His wife had made him go on a vacation to Europe two and a half months earlier, and there he'd been bitten by what he had thought was a stray dog.

"Slash is all right," Dunc said. "I got him with the butter knife at the same time I got you—and Death and Destruction. It didn't help the pit bulls, but Mr. Nerkovich is fine —the cops just thought it was all a student prank. That somebody had given him spiked punch or something."

Amos made a funny sound.

"What was that?" Dunc asked.

"It was a laugh. That's how a laugh sounds through gauze. I just remembered the first thing Slash said to me when he changed back into a human."

"What was that?"

"Before he knew where he was, naked with dogs all over him, he took a look at me and said: 'Binder, take a lap.' "

Dunc giggled. "Well there, you see— there *is* something funny about all this. Plus, you've got a new record."

"Record—what are you talking about?"

"Melissa. She actually hugged you. In the gym."

"Oh. Right. She thought I was a dog."

"That doesn't change it. She actually hugged you. Dog or not, that's a record."

"Well . . ."

"And speaking of records—I was reading an article the other day—"

"No."

"What do you mean, no? You haven't even heard what I was going to talk about."

"So all right, what was it?"

"It was an article about hang gliding—"

"No."

"It seems there isn't much of a distance record for hang gliding with two people—"

"No."

"So I've got this acquaintance who teaches hang gliding, and I thought we—"

"No."

"Amos—"

"No."

The Case of the Dirty Bird

When Dunc Culpepper and his best friend, Amos, first see the parrot in a pet store, they're not impressed—it's smelly, scruffy, and missing half its feathers. They're only slightly impressed when they learn that the parrot speaks four languages, has outlived ten of its owners, and is probably 150 years old. But when the bird starts mouthing off about buried treasure, Dunc and Amos get pretty excited—let the amateur sleuthing begin!

Dunc's Doll

Dunc and his accident-prone friend Amos are up to their old sleuthing habits once again. This time they're after a band of doll thieves! When a doll that once belonged to Charles Dickens's daughter is stolen from an exhibition at the local mall, the two boys put on their detective gear and do some serious snooping. Will a vicious watch dog keep them from retrieving the valuable missing doll?

Culpepper's Cannon

Dunc and Amos are researching the Civil War cannon that stands in the town square, when they find a note inside telling them about a time portal. Entering it through the dressing room of La Petite, a women's clothing store, the boys find themselves in downtown Chatham on March 8, 1862—the day before the historic clash between the *Monitor* and the *Merrimac*. But the Confederate soldiers they meet mistake them for Yankee spies. Will they make it back to the future in one piece?

Dunc Gets Tweaked

Best friends Dunc and Amos meet up with a new buddy named Lash when they enter the radical world of skateboard competition. When somebody "cops"—steals—Lash's prototype skateboard, the boys are determined to get it back. After all, Lash is about to shoot for a totally rad world's record! Along the way they learn a major lesson: *Never* kiss a monkey!

Dunc Breaks the Record

Best friends for life, Dunc and Amos have a small problem when they try hang gliding—they crash in the wilderness. Luckily, Amos has read a book about a boy who survived in the wilderness for fifty-four days. Too bad Amos doesn't have a hatchet. Things go from bad to worse when a wild man holds the boys captive. Can anything save them now?